First American Edition.
Copyright © 1995 The Walt Disney Company.
All rights reserved under international copyright
conventions. Published in the United States by
Grolier Enterprises, Inc., Danbury, Connecticut.
Originally published in Denmark as Robin Hood og
det store guldrøveri by Egmont Books,
Copenhagen, in 1994.

ISBN: 0-7172-8450-6
Manufactured in the United States of America

D   5 6 7 8

DISNEY'S
ROBIN HOOD
AND THE Great
Coach Robbery

GROLIER
BOOK CLUB EDITION

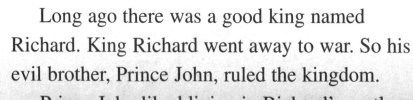

Long ago there was a good king named
Richard. King Richard went away to war. So his
evil brother, Prince John, ruled the kingdom.
Prince John liked living in Richard's castle.
He liked wearing Richard's crown.

But he liked Richard's gold most of all!
He had the royal soldiers guard the gold.

Prince John even slept with the gold.

He also shared his room with his servant,
Sir Hiss. Sir Hiss hissed whenever he talked—
and he talked all the time.

But most of the time, the prince was too
busy thinking about gold to listen to Sir Hiss.

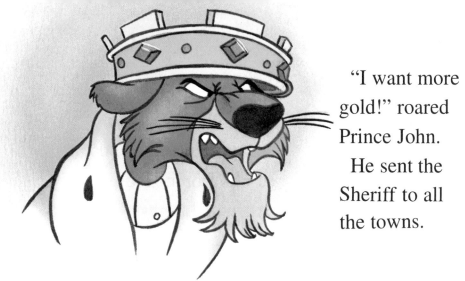

"I want more gold!" roared Prince John.

He sent the Sheriff to all the towns.

The people had to give him their last gold coins.

Soon the people were very poor. And Prince John was very rich!

But there was someone
who could help the poor.
His name was Robin Hood. He lived
in Sherwood Forest with his
band of merry men. Robin
and his men didn't like
what Prince John
was doing.

"People don't have
enough money to buy
food," said Robin's best
friend, Little John.

"We'll have to teach Prince John a lesson," replied Robin Hood.

So late one night,
Robin Hood and
Little John went to
the castle. They
waited for a cloud
to cover the moon.
Then they climbed
into the castle.

"The guards are asleep," whispered Robin Hood.
The two friends sneaked into Prince John's room.

Prince John and Sir Hiss were fast asleep, too.
"ZZZNORK-Hisss. ZZZNORK-Hisss,"
snored Sir Hiss.

Robin Hood and Little John took all
the gold they could carry.

The next day, Robin Hood and Little John
gave the gold back to the people. They told
them to buy food and clothes.

"Spend all the money," Robin said.
"Then the Sheriff won't be able to
take it back."

Prince John still had a lot of gold. But now
a little was missing. That made him very angry.
"Bandits are stealing my gold!" he shouted.

Prince John called for the Sheriff. He
told him to find the bandits.

"Search until you find them!"
Prince John ordered.

The Sheriff knew that Robin Hood was the thief.
So he and his soldiers searched Sherwood Forest.
They looked behind trees. They looked under bushes.
They looked everywhere except up!

Robin Hood and Little John were hiding in a tree!

The Sheriff couldn't find them anywhere, so he
returned to the castle.

Prince John decided he would get more gold by himself. The next day he went out in the royal coach. The poor people had to give their gold back to Prince John. Soon the royal treasure chest was filled with gold.

But Robin Hood and Little John were watching the prince. Robin had an idea.

"Come on, Little John, we need to change clothes," Robin said. The two friends raced back home.

Robin opened a trunk full
of old clothes. He gave Little
John a dress, a scarf, and a wig.
"Put these on," Robin said.

Little John didn't want to
wear a dress.
"Can't we just be
bandits?" he complained.
But he put on the
dress anyway.

Inside the royal coach, Prince John was playing with his gold. He was very happy.

"You have a talent for getting gold," Sir Hiss told him.

The greedy prince grinned. "You know what I always say: Rob the poor to feed the rich!" Prince John and Sir Hiss laughed and laughed.

Just then they heard someone calling.

"Yoo-hoo, Prince John! May I tell you your fortune?" cooed Robin Hood. He sounded just like an old woman.

Prince John loved to hear about himself. So he shouted, "Stop the coach!"

Sir Hiss didn't like the way the fortune-tellers looked. "What if they are bandits?" he whispered.

"Bandits in dresses? Really, Sir Hiss. You worry too much," the prince said.

Prince John
invited the fortune-tellers into
the royal coach. He let them kiss his royal hand.

So Robin and Little John stole the royal jewels
from the royal rings!

Sir Hiss saw
what happened,
but Prince John
did not.

Sir Hiss tried to warn Prince John. "Sire, did you see what they . . ."

"Sir Hiss, stop tickling my ear!" the prince snapped.

Prince John grabbed Sir Hiss and tied him in a knot.

"Sir Hiss, you have hissed your last hiss!" Prince
John shouted.

He stuffed Sir Hiss into a basket. Prince John put
a lid on the basket. Then he sat on the lid!

Robin Hood sat across from Prince John. He waved his hands. Then he called for the spirits to tell him Prince John's fortune.

"Yoo-hoo! Spirits! Come to us!" Robin said.

Little John was outside the coach. He held
a balloon on a stick. The balloon was full
of fireflies. When he heard Robin
call for the spirits, Little
John poked the
balloon through
the royal curtain.

"Look, Sire, look!" shouted Robin. "The spirits are here in a magic ball!"

"Floating spirits!" cried Prince John.

Robin looked into the balloon. "I see a face in the magic ball. It is a royal face. A kind, handsome, lovable, wise, and cuddly face."

"That's me," said Prince John.

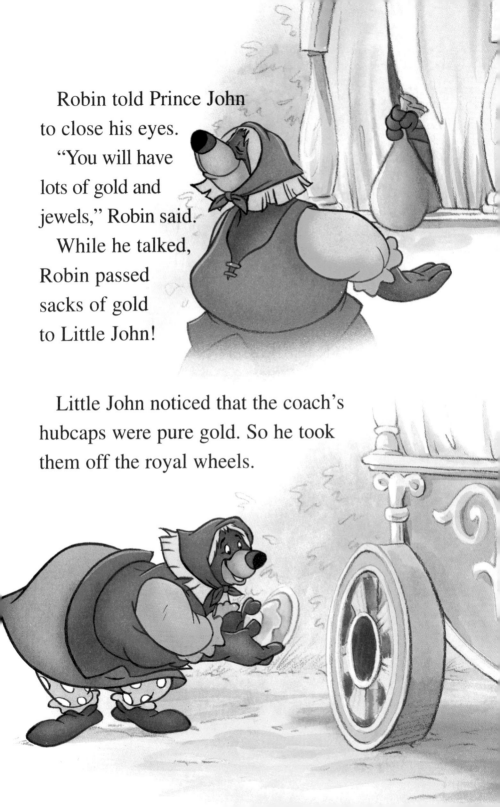

Robin told Prince John
to close his eyes.
"You will have
lots of gold and
jewels," Robin said.
While he talked,
Robin passed
sacks of gold
to Little John!

Little John noticed that the coach's
hubcaps were pure gold. So he took
them off the royal wheels.

While Robin was pretending to tell the
prince's fortune, Little John looked around.

"ZZZzzz.
ZZZzzz," snored
the royal guards.
They were all
fast asleep.
That gave
Little John
an idea!

He drilled
a hole in the
bottom of the
treasure chest.

CLINK-CLANK-CLINK-CLANK-CLINK!

The coins fell out through the hole. Little John took all the gold.

"ZZZzzz. ZZZzzz," snored the royal guards. They were still fast asleep.

Suddenly Robin Hood jumped out of the coach.
"We're off, Little John!" he shouted.

The two friends ran back into the forest.
They had the royal gold and the
royal jewels. Robin even had
the royal robe!

When Prince John opened his eyes, the
fortune-tellers were gone. And so were his gold,
his jewels, and even his robe. All Prince John
had left was his royal underwear!

"I've been robbed!" Prince John yelled. "After them, you fools!"

The royal coach bearers ran. But there were no hubcaps holding the wheels on, so the royal coach fell with a big CRASH!

Prince John and Sir Hiss went flying out of
the royal coach. They landed in a mud puddle
with a loud SPLAT!

"No, no, no!" Prince John cried when he saw the hole in the treasure chest. "Those bandits took all my gold!"

Sir Hiss hissed, "I knew this would happen. I tried to warn you, but you wouldn't listen."

"Be quiet," Prince John growled. "Or I'll tie you in another knot!"

Now Prince John was really angry. And he
stayed angry. Back at the castle, he yelled at
the Sheriff. "Get me the names of those bandits!"

"They are Robin Hood and Little John," said the Sheriff. "They are friends of the poor."

"They are outlaws!" Prince John shouted. "Find them and put them in jail!"

But that never happened.

Robin Hood and Little John went right on taking Prince John's gold and giving it back to the poor.

The poor people were grateful. They threw a party for Robin Hood and his friends.

And Robin Hood, Little John, and all the good people they helped lived happily ever after in Sherwood Forest.